Dear Parents and Educators,

Welcome to Penguin Young Readers! As parents and educators, you know that each child develops at their own pace—in terms of speech, critical thinking, and, of course, reading. Penguin Young Readers recognizes this fact. As a result, each Penguin Young Readers book is assigned a traditional easy-to-read level (1–4) as well as an F&P Text Level (A–P). Both of these systems will help you choose the right book for your child. Please refer to the back of each book for specific leveling information. Penguin Young Readers features esteemed authors and illustrators, stories about favorite characters, fascinating nonfiction, and more!

The Lucky Dogs
Penny and Clover, Follow That Ball!

LEVEL **1**

F&P TEXT LEVEL **D**

This book is perfect for an **Emergent Reader** who:
- can read in a left-to-right and top-to-bottom progression;
- can recognize some beginning and ending letter sounds;
- can use picture clues to help tell the story; and
- can understand the basic plot and sequence of simple stories.

Here are some **activities** you can do during and after reading this book:
- Word Repetition: Reread the story and count how many times you read the following words: *ball, bouncing, go, high, look, no*. Then, on a separate piece of paper, work with the child to write a new sentence for each word.
- Picture Clues: Sometimes, pictures can tell you something about the story that is not told in words. Have the child go through the book again and identify clues as to what the characters will find up the tree at the end of the story just by looking at the pictures.

Remember, sharing the love of reading with a child is the best gift you can give!

*This book has been officially leveled by using the F&P Text Level Gradient™ leveling system.

To dog people, cat people, and the
wonderful people (like Jenifer Marshall)
who have room in their hearts for both—ESP

For my friend Aitzi, because these
two puppies remind me of you—LM

PENGUIN YOUNG READERS
An Imprint of Penguin Random House LLC, New York

Text copyright © 2020 by Erica S. Perl.
Illustrations copyright © 2020 by Penguin Random House LLC. All rights reserved.
Published by Penguin Young Readers, an imprint of Penguin Random House LLC, New York.
Manufactured in China.

Visit us online at www.penguinrandomhouse.com.

Library of Congress Cataloging-in-Publication Data is available upon request.

ISBN 9781524793449 (pbk)   10 9 8 7 6 5 4 3 2 1
ISBN 9781524793456 (hc)   10 9 8 7 6 5 4 3 2 1

Penny and Clover, Follow That Ball!

by Erica S. Perl
illustrated by Leire Martín

Penny, look!

4

Go get the ball.

7

Oops!

Look out!

It hit the wall.

Bouncing high.

12

Bouncing low.

Bouncing ball,

where did you go?

No ball here.

No ball there.

No ball.

No ball anywhere.

Woof!

Woof!

Up the tree?

Climbing high,

I look and see.

Clover! Penny!

Look, you two.

The ball!

And also, someone new.